Rosie Jones

the

Orphan Girl

MARY DADA

ISBN 978-1-956001-09-9 (paperback)
ISBN 978-1-956001-10-5 (eBook)

Printed in the United States of America

Acknowledgement

I would like to thank God for giving me the ability to read and write. I would also like to thank my friends and family for making sure I get my writing done and always being therefor me. Lastly, I would like to thank my teacher Mrs Murphy for always checking my stories and making sure they made sense.

First book of Series: Rosie Jones

Chapter 1

My life is somehow fun without my parents, It's fun not knowing who they are but I do wonder why they didn't want me...

I am Rosie Jones and this is my story. I am not going to start with when I was born because it's a bit boring. Alii can say is, my birthday is May 3rd. I am 10 years old. Alii know about my parents is that my mum was 17 when she had me. Pretty young, right? And my dad was 30, how strange is that? My dad didn't care about me when I was born; he wanted nothing to do with me and my mum. So now I am here in care but when my mum put me into care she left a note. I was only allowed to read it on my 10th birthday:

Hi Rosie,

I am sorry I can't stay with you and I am not here with you. I am alive if you're wondering, but you probably wouldn't care after what I did to you. I left you at the Joy Smith Care home because I needed to continue with school life and go to University. I didn't expect you, sorry Rosie, but I didn't. So, when I had you, I explained to Aunt Joy (the head of the care home) that I couldn't take care of you and go to school at the same time. So Aunt Joy took you in and agreed to raise you up as her child. Hopefully, when I graduate from university, get a job, buy a house and sort my life out, I will come back for you. I promise.

LoveMumxx

Chapter 2

Aunt Joy woke me up by spraying everyone with apple juice. She can be nice when she wants to but she is also really mean. I share a room with 3 girls; Elizabeth, Jane and

Poppy. My friend is Poppy but Elizabeth and Jane always bully me. Out of both of them who do I hate? Both of them. They always bully me because my mum had me at a really young age.

"Wakey wakey, rise and shine," sang Aunt Joy throwing pillows everywhere. "Your social workers are coming so wear something smart and clean this room,"

Aunt Joy continued. My social worker is called Abigail she is really nice and friendly because she gives me sweets, buys me the latest clothes and branded shoes. She is also very easy to talk to. Today I am wearing a black pencil skirt, pink blouse and some Nike air forces. I am going to see when my appointment is because I wanted to go to shops with Poppy so we can buy some breakfast and some other things as well. As I left the room, Jane and Elizabeth shouted "Rosie we hate you!"

Chapter 3

Aunt Joy told me that my appointment was at 12pm So I have 3 hours to have fun with Poppy. "Poppy lets go now!" I screamed. We got on the 295 bus and stopped at Berry Lane and entered McDonalds, I ordered pancakes with syrup and a chocolate muffin. Poppy ordered a triple chocolate cookie and a bacon roll. The lady that served us was neat and helpful and was really friendly to us. By the time Poppy and I finished eating we had 2 hours left so we first went to the park. When we had finished at the park, we entered Greggs, I bought orange juice and a sausage roll, so did Poppy.

When we had finished enjoying our self at Berry Lane. We went home and Poppy's appointment had just started. I still had to wait for 30 minutes. I spent that half an hour stealing Elizabeth and Jane's clothes and putting them in secret places.

Chapter 4

I am sitting outside Aunt Joy's office while my social worker is inside talking with her. I have to wait for five minutes and it is going to be the most terrifying five minutes of my life. The door opened and my heart started to pound.

"Rosie it's your turn," said Aunt Joy, as Poppy left the room. I entered nervously and Abigail ushered me into a seat.

"Rosie I have some amazing news for you, it could actually change your life," explained Abigail.

"Really! What?" I replied eagerly.

"A family is ready to adopt you." exclaimed Aunt Joy. "Seriously," I said surprisingly.

"YES!" bellowed Aunt Joy and Abigail together. At that point I just remembered I had a letter from my mum inside my pocket and I looked at the top of the envelope which read:

A letter from murn please read

But in the letter it's says:

"When I graduate from university, get a job, buy a house and sort my life out I will come back for you."

It's been 10 whole years now where are you, Mum?

After I had finished day dreaming and looking at the top of the envelope, I muttered to myself "She is not coming back, so let's meet this family that wants to adopt me." After talking to myself I immediately answered "I would love to meet them."

Abigail quickly replied before I could change my mind "Nice choice, Rosie. You can meet them tomorrow at 11 O'clock, be ready in the morning."

Chapter 5

Aunt Joy woke me up by pulling my legs, "Its 9 O'clock," I yawned.

"Yes, I need to make sure you look marvellous when you go to the adopting family," replied Aunt Joy

"But I have 2 hours until I need to go, why now?" I complained.

"Because we are going out to get your nails, hair and makeup done," chatted Aunt Joy

"Fine!" I shouted, feeling excited and apprehensive.

I wore a black top, pink leggings and a pair of sandals. had waffles for breakfast. After I finished eating, I entered Aunt Joy's car and we drove past Berry Lane and entered the motorway. We spent 30 minutes on the motorway and finally exited to Abbey Lane. We stopped at a shop called Mr Right; it had things to do with nails, makeup and hairstyles. Aunt Joy led me into the shop and a woman called Susan said "Hello! Welcome to Mr Right, how can I help you?"

"Hello I am Joy and this Rosie, is it possible to have Rosie's makeup, hair and nails done?" asked Aunt Joy.

"Yes it's possible," said Susan.

"So how long would it take?" Questioned Aunt Joy. "One hour," replied Susan.

Aunt Joy left the shop waving goodbye to me. Susan commanded "Enter one of the showers and when you are done I'll start painting your nails for you!" After I had finished showering Susan gave me some clothes to wear, a pink dress and a pair of Addidas shoes. She started to paint my nails pink, put my hair into a pony tail and applied red lipstick and mascara on to my face. "Wow you look amazing!" Screamed Aunt Joy "Rosie I forgot to tell you the family that's wants to adopt you; their name is Smith."

"Oh ok thanks Aunt Joy," I said. Aunt Joy paid Susan extra and we drove to the Smith Family wondering what they will be like.

Chapter 6

When we arrived at the Smith family I was greeted by their daughter (who was 8 years old). Her name was Holly. "Hello Rosie, I am Mr Smith you can call me Daniel," said Mr Smith. "I am Destiny," interrupted Mrs Smith, "Come in Rosie," said Mr Smith.

The house had four floors it was massive inside. It had 3 bathrooms, 6 bedrooms, 3 study areas,1 big office, a gigantic kitchen and a huge living room.

"Rosie can you please come to my room?" begged Holly. "Sure why not" I replied walking up the stairs with Holly.

When we were upstairs Holly said, "My mum told me why you're here today. I hope you like it here."

We played dress up for 10 minutes and Holly's mum called us downstairs because she had finished making lunch. The whole table was full of food like roast potatoes, vegetables, water, two whole chickens and a triple chocolate fudge cake. Aunt Joy was so surprised when she saw how much food were on the table. We all took our spaces around the table; I ate a piece of chicken with roast potatoes and some vegetables by the side. I couldn't have pudding because I was too full, so Mrs Smith cut half of the pudding and put it into a bag for me so that I could take it home.

After we all finished eating, Mrs Smith cleaned all the plates, Aunt Joy and Mr Smith went inside the office and Holly took me on a tour around the house. She showed me a plain white room and Mrs Smith said "If you do decide that you want us to adopt you then this will be your room," The room had a big wardrobe, a bathroom to myself, a study area with a laptop on the desk and a king size bed. I really liked this family.

Once Aunt Joy had finished with the paperwork it was time for me to go. I hugged Holly and Mrs Smith and shook Mr Smith's hand firmly.

"I hope you've enjoyed yourself Rosie?" asked Mrs Smith. "I have really enjoyed myself," I answered.

"I hope to see you again," said Mrs Smith.

"Me too," I replied.

"Well, you will be seeing each other again at a picnic. I won't be there to supervise," announced Aunt Joy.

"Yes a picnic!" I shouted. I waved goodbye as I entered the car and we drove home.

Chapter 7

When we got home Aunt Joy whispered into my ear "The picnic is tomorrow."

"What time do I need to be there for?" I asked. "Around 1 O'clock." answered Aunt Joy.

"Thanks Aunt Joy," I said opening the front door. When I entered my room I saw Poppy writing in her dairy, "Hi Poppy," I said.

"Oh Rosie you're back, hello," she answered.

"How was the family you went to see today?" asked Poppy. "Really good I love them and what are you doing?" I questioned.

"I am just writing in my dairy," answered Poppy.

"That's good, I am going downstairs, bye." I said

I left the room and went downstairs to see who I could find. I saw Elizabeth playing games on the computer, "Hey Rosie!" she shouted "Where did you go today?"

"Nowhere," I muttered.

I heard Aunt Joy shouting, "Dinner is ready!"

I walked across hallway to the kitchen, there were pasta, meatballs and special sauce on the table but I couldn't eat it because I was still full from all that yummy food at Holly's house so I ate my triple chocolate fudge cake instead. When I had finished eating, I got my clothes ready for the picnic tomorrow and went to bed early.

I woke up at 9 O'clock and played on my phone until my stomach began to rumble. So I went downstairs to the kitchen to cook my breakfast. I made peppered fried egg with some toast and a hot cup of tea. After I had finished eating, I went upstairs to the bathroom, took a bubble bath and wore my picnic clothes which was a multicoloured dress along with a pair of sandals. Then it was time for me to go to the park (which was 10 minutes away).

When I got there I saw Holly, Mrs Smith and Mr Smith sitting on a bench waiting for me.

"Hi." I said walking up to them.

"Hello Darling," Mrs Smith said "Nice to see you again." I sat down and Holly opened the picnic basket and Mrs Smith laid out the plates and the food. The food today wasn't as much as yesterday. They had 4 different kinds of sandwiches, 4 chocolate cookies, a vanilla cake, 2 bottles of water and 2 bottles of orange juice. After eating, Holly and I played in the park on the swings. When I was swinging I saw one of my mum's friends (her name was Amanda). I remembered her because she used to take me out to places on my birthday since my mum didn't want to take me because she was always busy.

"Hello Rosie," said Amanda. "Hi." I answered.

Mr and Mrs Smith walked into the park and they asked together "Rosie, are you okay?"

"Yes I am fine." I replied.

"Who are these people Rosie?" asked Amanda. "They are going to adopt me," I responded happily.

"Oh Okay, let's take a picture of all of us," asked Amanda. "I want to remember this moment." "Sure." I said.

A member of the public took a picture of all of us. Holly stood next to me while Mr and Mr Smith stood at the back with Amanda. After taking the picture,

Aunt Joy's car pulled up to the car park driveway and we met Aunt Joy near the entrance.

"Hello Rosie, do you want to get adopted by the Smith family?" asked Aunt Joy.

"Yes please," I answered. "Yes Sister!" screamed Holly.

"Rosie you know your birthday is tomorrow there is going to be a leaving party tomorrow on your birthday," said Aunt Joy.

"Lucky me thank you Aunt Joy. Bye Holly, Mr Smith and Mrs Smith see you very soon."

As I entered the car Aunt Joy told me, "I put two of your suitcases and some cardboard boxes into your room so you can start packing,"

"Thank you Aunt Joy" I said, hugging her.

Chapter 8

When I got home I went straight to my room to start packing. I first packed my clothes into my suitcase, then my shoes into a big cardboard box, I put all my toys in the other cardboard box and my hair accessories into my second suitcase. After I had finished packing my bag, I went downstairs to Aunt Joy to ask her if she knew where everyone was.

"Aunt Joy where is everyone?" I questioned.

"Well... I am not supposed to tell you this, but everyone is out shopping for your birthday (which is tomorrow) they are getting your birthday present, your birthday cake and some decorations that we can put around the house, you promise you won't tell the others I told you?" answered Aunt Joy.

"I promise," I said happily.

After talking with Aunt Joy I went back upstairs to my room to continue with my packing. When I was done, I heard the front door open. So, I ran downstairs and I saw Poppy, Elizabeth and Jane holding a few boxes and bags, I wondered what was inside those bags and boxes.

"Poppy!" I called helping to carry the boxes into Aunt Joy's room. "What are you getting me for my birthday?" I inquired.

"Something special," Poppy replied "Anyway let's go to bed, Rosie. You have a big day tomorrow," Poppy continued.

"Yes I do, I am leaving here finally and I am turning 11," I said. "Goodnight Poppy," I said climbing into bed.

Chapter 9

I was woken by Aunt Joy and Poppy singing to me the birthday song.

"Thank you," I replied when they had finish singing.

"Rosie, I got you these clothes. It's not your birthday present from me but just a gift." Poppy said.

"Thank you so much! These clothes are really fashionable," I said hugging her.

I took a special shower and wore the clothes that Poppy bought for me. She bought me a pink dress from River Island, a big birthday badge, a best friend bracelet and a pair of high heels.

After getting myself ready I decided to go downstairs to start my party in the living room. Elizabeth, Jane, Poppy and Aunt Joy were putting up the last bits of the decorations. I was surprised to see the two evil witches Elizabeth and Jane helping out.

"Hi Elizabeth, why are you and Jane helping out for my party, I thought we are enemies?" I asked.

"I am only helping because I will probably never see you again and I thought we could stop fighting and become friends. I am sorry Rosie for everything I have done to you."

"I am sorry too," I said.

After declaring that I, Elizabeth and Jane were now friends. Aunt Joy opened the front door and Holly, Mr Smith and Mrs Smith came through the door with lots of present and party food that Mrs Smith had cooked for my birthday.

"Hello Holly, Mr Smith and Mrs Smith, nice to see you here," I said.

"Happy birthday Rosie!" Holly screamed handing me my present.

"Thank you Holly," I said giving her a friendly hug.

"Rosie, can you take me to your kitchen so I can put some food there?" asked Mrs Smith.

"Yes! Of course."

I led Mrs Smith into the kitchen and after that I went back to the living room to start dancing. I danced for 30 minutes and there was a faint knock on the door. I ran to the door hoping it was someone good. When I opened the door, there was a strange woman standing there...

Chapter 10

"Rosie?" she questioned. "Yes," I answered. "Hello Rosie, Happy birthday." Said the strange woman.

"Thank you. How do you know my name?" I said awkwardly.

"I know your name because I know who you are." Answered the strange woman.

Aunt Joy called from behind the living room door "Rosie who's at the door? We are waiting for you to open your present."

"Urn... Aunt Joy I'm not sure who's here I think you should come." I replied nervously.

"Sure." Aunt Joy said pushing the living room door open and rushing over to me.

"Amy! You're not supposed to be here!" said Aunt Joy furiously, "You need to contact me before hand and let me know you want to come,".

"What's wrong Joy, I am only here for my daughter's birthday."

"Wait... Is she my mum?" I asked anxiously.

"Yes! I am darling."

"No, No, No," I said running upstairs with tears coming down my face.

"Rosie!" I heard Poppy shout as I closed the door behind me.

I sat in my room for 10 minutes crying my eyes out and I heard a small knock on the door. The door opened and Poppy sat down beside me.

"Your mum is in Aunt Joy's office. She can go if you want," said Poppy.

"I don't know what I want. It's been 10 years and she decides to come now."

"I know how you feel Rosie but you've got to talk to her." "Fine!" I shouted "I'll go speak to her now."

Chapter 11

I ran downstairs and knocked on Aunt Joy's office door with a THUD!

"Yes!" I heard Aunt Joy reply.

I opened the door slowly and saw Aunt Joy typing on her computer and my mum texting on her phone.

"Urn... Aunt Joy can I please talk to my mum in private." I asked politely.

"Yes sure," Aunt Joy said packing up some of her folders and going out the door.

After Aunt Joy had left, there was an awkward silence for five minutes and my mum finally said.

"Rosie, this is your birthday present." When I opened it there were a pair of diamond earrings that I had really wanted for a long time.

"Thanks mum," I said hugging her nervously.

"Mum... I just wanted to ask, why did you decide to come now? It's been 10 years, you had lots of chances to come and collect me but you didn't?" I questioned awkwardly.

"Well, Rosie. You remember Amanda and the picture you took with her when you went to the park. Amanda sent it to me and told me where she saw you. I was really angry when I heard about it. I thought you might be leaving on your birthday and that's why I am here."

"So you're not ready to take me home," I said with anger beginning to build inside me.

"Darling, there's a lot to do first before I can take you back and I am not ready. I just came here to ask Aunt Joy if she can keep you here a bit longer until I am ready."

"WHEN ARE YOU GOING TO BE READY?" I shouted. "Weill am going to get adopted by the Smith family and there's nothing you can do about it. Get out of here mum I don't want to see you again," I continued.

I left Aunt Joy's office and went back to the living room to meet everyone. As I entered the living room, I heard the front door close and I guessed that it was my mum. In the living room everyone was talking amongst themselves until they noticed me through the doorway.

"Rosie, Aunt Joy said. Where is your mum?"

"She's gone. I told her that I wanted to be adopted." I answered.

"Alright. You go and continue with your party if you feel you can," said Aunt Joy.

I opened all my presents, cut my cake, ate all the food and said goodbye to everyone. I couldn't believe my birthday was over. What a day it has been I thought to myself. I went upstairs and I put all my presents in my empty suitcase and fell soundly asleep dreaming about tomorrow.

Chapter 12

I woke up really early in the morning and I took all my suitcases and bags downstairs and I placed them next to the front door. I heard Aunt Joy in the kitchen moving a few pots and pans. I opened the kitchen door and Aunt Joy had just finished cooking my breakfast. I took a seat at the table with Aunt Joy. While we were eating, we discussed what was going to happen today.

After eating I said to Aunt Joy "Thank you. The food was delicious, and I loved it."

"Aww thanks Rosie you just made my day," replied Aunt Joy.

"It's alright," I said calmly.

After chatting with Aunt Joy, I went back upstairs to take my shower. As I went back to my room to get changed, I heard Poppy yawning and I saw her sitting on her bed waiting for me.

"Hi Poppy," I said running up to her on the bed and giving her a hug.

"Hello Rosie, I hope you have finished packing and I hope you are ready to go."

"I am ready, but I am going to miss you," I said feeling broken inside.

"I know I am going to miss you too, but you've got to go." "Yes, I've got to go," I said.

I left Poppy alone and got changed into a red jumpsuit and wore a pair of sandals. After changing, I heard a BEEP! From outside and I knew it was time for me to go.

"Poppy it's time for me to go," I said sadly.

"Yes Rosie, good luck and goodbye." Poppy said with tears forming in her eyes.

I closed the door behind me, and rushed downstairs. I gleefully asked, "Are they here?"

"Oh yes they are here," said Aunt Joy with her voice changing into a sad tone.

Aunt Joy helped to load all my things inside Mr Smith's boot and I gave her a last goodbye hug. I entered the car and we drove off to my new life. I wonder what the future will hold.

osie Jones is just a normal 10 year old girl who lives in an orphanage. She has never met her mother. BUT, today she turns 11 and things are about to change for her...

Mary Dada is a talented author!

'You'd be silly to miss out on this amazing book—Mary's first novel'